PRAISE FOR
AND S

GW01395975

'Heartfelt but clear-
    this is a powerful and moving collection by a
    remarkable poet writing in extremis.'
        —Peter Sansom

'More than a distilled exploration of the
mechanisms and processes of grief, here is a
sequence of elegies that double as love poems,
dissecting with painstaking precision a long and
complex relationship. Shot through with Pimlott's
trademark combination of the quotidian and
transcendent, this musical and metaphor-rich work
will – in the best possible way – break your heart.'
        —Jacqueline Saphra

AFTER THE RITES AND SANDWICHES

Poems by Kathy Pimlott

THE EMMA PRESS

For Robert (1953-2021)
without whom

ℭ

THE EMMA PRESS

First published in the UK in 2024 by The Emma Press Ltd.
Poems © Kathy Pimlott 2024.
Cover artwork © Mark Andrew Webber 2024.

All rights reserved.

The right of Kathy Pimlott to be identified as the author
of this work has been asserted in accordance with the
Copyright, Designs and Patents Act 1988.

ISBN 978-1-915628-32-9

A CIP catalogue record of this book
is available from the British Library.

Edited and typeset by Emma Dai'an Wright.

Printed and bound in the UK
by the Holodeck, Birmingham.

The Emma Press
theemmapress.com
hello@theemmapress.com
Birmingham, UK

CONTENTS

Prologue: First Date

Imagine we stand on a rope bridge over the canyon, where rhododendrons cling to crevices, daring the corsairs to sever the ropes with their scimitars, sipping cocktails that don't make us any drunker than we are. It's sunset. From somewhere down below, a small orchestra and mid-career soprano render Strauss's *Four Last Songs*, which makes the corsairs weep until tears roll down their tattooed forearms. This lasts for an hour, no sudden nightfall, no bats. The corsairs exhaust themselves. Chastened, they return to their three-masted galleon anchored in the bay. How very lovely the sky – that tenderness before light dies.

No shock advised

It's cruel work
to kneel down
and hunch over
a so-familiar body at the foot of the stairs and

press hard with the heels of
your interlocked hands
singing in gasps
to a rhythm that's fled
each push rippling and rocking the belly fat

to take turns to stand stock-still in an icy fire and not run but

stay put and listen from the kitchen
as the serious strangers
arrive and fail and fail again
to kindle a tick that might
be coaxed to catch hold and

over and over
the defibrillator says
no shock advised
because there's nothing
to be done

and it's done

but how still the sweet mad hopeful brain insists
it will be ok ok ok

How to be a widow

I do two of the just-one-things the radio doctor
promises will make a difference: drink water
and balance on one leg with my eyes closed.

I've written my menu for the week. Today's chowder.
I manage ten pieces of the 1000 piece jigsaw's scenes
from Jane Austen. Tomorrow I'll visit friends and say

it's alright, really, it's alright, seventy, eighty percent
alright, their condolences in quote marks, "sad loss",
"tragic accident", little pegs pinning the laundered fact

to the line, blood-streaked mucusy froth washed out.
Because who wants to talk about death? No-one.
Not while the world's burning. Him as lost glacier,

landscape cracked into vast spaces, the loss of all
my excuses. I was on the phone, then peeling potatoes,
then scrubbing a tea-stained mug and then he was dead.

Who wants to hear about the colours? Normal, then purple
then grey in a moment like the sea changing as light
shifts with the clouds. No-one. Colonies are collapsing.

Children have taken to the streets with semi-automatic guns.
Words no longer hold and I've been picked up and dropped
into a foreign land in which everywhere looks the same.

What I said to the two policewomen: do you want tea?
Someone radios someone. Someone calls them back.
Someone has found a wad of new bank notes on our street.

What I said to the paramedic: yes, I moved his legs.
No, no beat as we took turns to try to bring him back,
husband, dad. We stand and sit in our kitchen, open windows

flooded with noise: people at pub tables, drinking, losing cash.
At moments I feel I might step over him at the foot of the stairs,
run up Tottenham Court Road, along Euston Road, into the park.

It gets dark. All we want to do is lie down or scream
but we make conversation with the officers from 6 until 11,
say it's odd he didn't swear as he fell, being very sweary.

We stand and sit in the kitchen, wait for it to be otherwise.
It isn't. The mug with the tea stains was that one on which
Alice tucks a flamingo under her arm, gets on with the match.

Death Admin I

Your demise constitutes a quarter off council tax;
the removal of a vote you seldom cast and then
only to be contrary; write-off of a modest overdraft;
the bill for an overpaid pension. Tell Us Once promises
it will be a doddle. It is not. I repeat time and again
in spoken and in written words to the indifferent
or distracted: *He has died. What do I need to do?*

After the rites and sandwiches

We haven't yet drawn the heavy curtains
on the navy sky. A window is open
to let night air into the flickering room
where, unusually gathered, we sit distracted
by television from the churn of ifs and whys.

A moth flies in, an ordinary moth, attracted
to the lamp. It zig-zags round the room,
the *flying crooked* of the poem I've just read
at your funeral, the one I told you I would read
that time we saw swifts at the old reservoir.

Infected by its madcap flapping, we flap, attempt
to guide it back out. Despite us, it finds its way
into the lamp's bowl where, from underneath,
I see how, in the heat, its trembling wings begin
to flake away until it stills, its outline a motif

etched into the glass. Some might say it's you,
restless, returned, not as Graves' cabbage white
but as another flitting thing. I don't, though just now
even a flimsy moth is weighty. Trying to settle
into thoughtless torpor, I can't help but feel the blame.

Death Admin II

It shouldn't be a surprise, the weight, the quantity.
Not knowing what to expect, I take my pink rucksack,
carry you home again all down Holborn on my back,
looking like a sensible woman out for a day trip.
I stow you at the back of your half of the wardrobe
among the various kits and short-sleeved cotton shirts
while I have a think about what to do with you.

At the crem there is a garden of standard roses
in rows, like a parade, a little army of remembrance.
That wouldn't do for one who never could stay in line.
Almost everywhere is illegal but England must be
covered in ashes heaped in tenderly chosen spots.
Will there be fragments of bone? There's certainly
too much for just one place and I'm thinking

of all the places I might leave a little of your residue:
the glorious mimosa in Regent's Park, hollow tree
on the Heath, Cheltenham's raucous finishing post,
Brighton Pier, a Cornish cliff or flat wide beach
under a castle, places we, the left-behind, might visit
with or without you. I won't say any words. No point.
You can't listen and I've had enough of talking to myself.

The mimosa was starting to colour last time I passed.
I looked to see how I might do it, step over the planting,
vinca, hellebores, how I might need water to wash you
into the hard soil. But first I have to open the plastic urn
and scoop out some of you. With a spoon? How will that be?
The Heath is a bus ride away, 24, Pimlico to South End Green.
It could be the hollow tree where our girls and all the children

climbed in to be inside the magic, or the path where each year
we picked sloes, you always reaching for more than we needed.
Or at glad Brighton Pier, not into the sea but among the noise
of the machines, ding of the pinball, clatter of the penny falls,
in a stripy paper bag, lodged in a crevice between the boards
(though gulls might tweak at you), behind the deckchair stacks,
or quietly sown in the Horror Hotel. I need to think it through.

There isn't a ghost

but if there were, it wouldn't be lurking
at the foot of the staircase but tapping
on windows of parked-up police vans
hissing *Turn off your bloody engine*

or pouring praise for his homesick song
in the gummy ear of the local street drunk.
If there were a ghost it wouldn't be half seen
in the sad nightlight of the refrigerator

but among the squashes, beguiling the ladies
with the perfume of a perfect tarte aux pommes,
the skin rasp of a loofah, or a piquant memory
of Toshiro Mifune's gait. There isn't a ghost

though if there were it wouldn't be wailing
woefully but running like wild fire, burning
one scheme after another into piles of ash.
You can look and look but there isn't a ghost.

And then that first Christmas

Of this, our first Christmas away from ourselves
as we were, what can I say? No-one wants to think
about the way, just like that, a person becomes meat.

December was a race to tick off the dark, draw curtains
at four, weigh the bother of needles against the cheer
of small lights reflecting off spectacles and fancy flutes,

making a facsimile of joy. The story we keep going
teeters in the fug of many breaths in an overheated room,
febrile with possible distress, saved by homely protocols

which lead us to tables pushed together and dressed,
cracker hats, the pudding's song. Everyone wants
to be laughing, happy for each other and themselves.

We explain our careful choices of presents or despair
in vouchers when imagination failed under the weight
of absence – no-one contesting the way to ignite brandy,

the acceptable time to start drinking, no-one to brace the day
against sinking under so much good stuff, no-one to excuse,
let go early, while it's still in full swing, upstairs to sleep it off.

Interior décor

I bought that turquoise throw to liven up the room.
They used it to cover you, make things almost normal,
as though you might have lain down naked on your back
on the draughty hall floor and needed its little warmth,

its modesty. Everyone has at least one beautiful part
which stays beautiful even when the rest of them
falls to ruin. For you, for me, it was your hands.
Before they called time, they asked if we'd like

to say goodbye and, though we knew you'd been gone
from the start, we left the airlock of the kitchen –
wife, daughter – to kneel one each side and weep
over your hands, like a Renaissance Lamentation.

I think what we want of love is to be made beautiful:
your almost green eyes, ridiculously dainty ear lobes,
that muscle V to groin. First sight? I don't recall.
But the easy way you lifted unloved children in the home

and swung them up until they screamed and begged
to be put down, then begged you to do it again, again,
made you seem like someone I could make a life, make
loved children with. There was no blood on the throw,

so I folded it, replaced it on the couch. When I get cold
these evenings, I may lay my hand where it rests but I wrap
the yellow rug round my legs as I watch a flickering world
paint portraits, garden, choose wedding frocks despite it all.

Looking for a cure in parks and gardens

We're out and about, looking to lull that bully, anxiety.
Everywhere there are small wildernesses. Fleabane creeps
in shallow earth. A shock of buttercups. By contrast

the Rose Garden is all bud and labels promising grace,
good days to come: *Peace, Joie de Vivre, Open Arms,*
while back at home squirrels pick over a litter of petals

shattered by last night's rain and in the jokey birdhouse –
ridiculous, mullioned, thatched – there are perhaps
a dozen chicks, each piping for the day's caterpillars.

Grass is electric from the downpour. Flies are busy
about the succulent corpse of a slug. Forget-me-nots
are all but over and, close by, one dapper magpie rattles,

side-eyed, bides its time. Back in the park, an earnest group
takes notes, discusses light, soil pH. Your people, I say,
throwing up a trellis for the untethered tendrils of my dear girl,

the untethered tendrils which I failed to wind or wound
too tight. Too much is happening. Perhaps ferns will be balm.
Steady, they've hardly changed over unimaginably deep time.

Since you fell downstairs and died

I've eaten many squares of chocolate with the conviction
that it's good for me, something to do with the blood.
The weather's promised but no-show ferocious interludes

disappoint me. I want to be grabbed by the scruff, shaken
till my teeth rattle even though our dentist's retired.
The new ones are efficient. They've removed you from the files.

I've taken to lists to just this side of crazy to keep sane.
Socks in bed are a comfort. Forgive me, I've laughed,
glided lightly round garden centres, sipped fizzy wine

with friends, sorted out edge pieces of puzzles. And I sleep
most nights, the kind of sleep people dream of, unbroken,
many-fathomed, waking with the light. It's tidier.

The onion skins you trailed from kitchen to living room
are no longer an issue but the if-onlys, a parade of fresh recruits
marching for no obvious purpose, bother me. And the if-I'd-justs

in red coats, mounted on dark horses. Not one drops a rifle
or stumbles against the shiny heel of the one in front, not one
falls to their knees on the compacted dust. It breaks my heart.

Stuffed Monkey

from Jane Grigson's English Food

It's impossible to foretell what will provoke tears, the sort
that well up and tip over while you hold onto the kitchen sink
waiting for them to subside.

It could be a bunch of keys, so many of them mysterious
from down the years, or clippings in a wallet, its leather
soft-shaped to a back pocket.

Or this cook book, *English Food*, sellotaped, cover missing,
pages stained, translucent with greasy butter prints,
the voice instructive, calm.

Tucked in, there's a scrap scrawled with a list of ingredients
for just the filling of a classic lemon tart.
He didn't need instructions

for its pâte sablé case, having mastered pastry: sweet crust,
short crust, rough puff, choux, all the many variations.
And, here, Stuffed Monkey,

which no-one has ever had – before he made it,
shiny with egg white glaze, round, heavy and dark
from brown sugar and cinnamon.

So plain to look at, so dense, delicious and unknown.
Now I follow the steps, the book propped open,
method a bit vague. And I'm crying.

I could say widowhood, regret, could say it's just a layer
of peel and ground almonds between two discs
of something like a pastry dough.

Jane says to make the dough '*as if* you are making pastry.'
I think she means rubbing in with fingertips, bringing together.
I could say '*as if* I'm suddenly so specifically lonely.'

Baked and cooled, the Stuffed Monkey sits in the shallow tin
which held our Christmas biscuits, stolid, a good traveller,
waiting to be taken somewhere. Sure of a welcome.

What I do with you now you're dead

The Queen is dead too and on her way to a proper tomb.
Everything's shut and there's nothing on tv, but the sun
comes out so I go to the mimosa tree where, months ago,
I dumped, in a laughing panic, dumped, about a quarter
of your ashes and ran away, the illicit thrill exactly what
you would have wanted. Today, with a flask, shortbread,

I've come because, while I don't love the Queen, it seems
like a fitting thing to do. This royal park is empty, quiet,
allowing me to cry all through its splendid long borders
with their harmonious purple and blue planting until,
on a near-enough bench, I sit. By my feet, Lamb's Ears
offer silky comfort, as does the pile of pistachio shells,

little coracles, showing someone sat here eating a bagful.
You kept your shells in the pockets of your gardening coat
which I emptied out before taking it to the charity shop
with your best shoes. The mimosa's not out of course
but its ferny leaves show promise of the glory to come.
A robin perches closer than he should, inspects me,

then accepts a crumb or two. Your ashes have disappeared,
no longer so alarmingly burnt-bone visible, so very there.
They say the old Queen's coffin is oak, lined with lead;

three-quarters of you is still in the back of the wardrobe.
A crow chases off my robin. So much peril. It's enough
to be sitting thumbing Lamb's Ears, thinking about you.

The sort of thing we did together of a Sunday

It's a perfect day for raptors on the marshes, heat rising,
oceans of sky. The reeds sport seed tassels, copper and pink,
susurrate concealing warblers and bunting, those small birds
we don't really know.

But we do know raptors:
sparrowhawk, peregrine, kestrel and the big one, marsh harrier,
their command.

I look so hard so long all I can see are floaters,
like pollywogs in the ditches where piles of fat frogs sunbathe,
their tremendous thighs beautifully hinged, while the boatmen
cast shadows and ripples which belie

their weightlessness.
Dragonflies or azure damselflies conjoin,

fly or quiver coupled.
All that's missing is the endless hiss of cicadas
and it could be the Camargue –

if you keep your eyes away
from the horizon's highspeed line and the Dartford Crossing.

There are worse places to be on this hot blue-sky day
than opposite Erith where the sails of dinghies lend a glamour.

Five seals bask on the far bank by an outlet creek,
seals, not rubbish sacks as we'd first thought.

The old army shooting range's metal numbers endure,
like Hollywood, a bit battered but only 4 is missing.

A board says this is where raptors perch when resting,
cast their unearthly sight over yellow anthills, boardwalks,
the hides' flapped windows,

                              rushes and willow.

What are we doing here beyond our Freedom Pass limit?
Sunday walking.
Far enough,   on the flat,   somewhere
there's more sky than anything,

somewhere big enough
                to contain all we won't bring up
        to spoil our lovely day.

Not like that

I watched you lay waste to the night staff.
One day you arrived in furious tears. One night
you found me inconsolable from that film by Sajit Ray.
It felt like intimacy.

Everyone loved us, called us Whiplash Wanda
and the Sunshine Kid, gave us homes for all but free,
filled skips with treasures for us. We were stardust.
We sold yoghurt in Camden Lock.

If you don't ask for much what you're given
is sumptuous. I found the roses you'd hidden,
not for me. This was not the first time nor the last.
I should've snapped the heads off

not put them back. I thought of many vengeful acts
but didn't enact them, well, hardly any, heard you
tell someone not to worry, *she's not like that.*
Years later, I think

there's a wrinkle of suspicion in the officer's mind
that I'd pushed you down the stairs. I don't blame him,
that's his job. But I'm not and never was like that.
It's tangled, we were careless,

lazy, generous, kind in almost all ways. There's more
but things have sunk to what's the point? The porch light
flicks on, just enough to sort out the right key to get me in,
milk on the turn, bread hardening.

The Passing Visit

A friend came by from Brussels and we talked of our dead
or rather about what they leave behind, the stuff in storage,

the binding strands. I told him more than I'd told most,
of how (and I said, then rejected, the word *tumultuous*),

how *textured* our long, long marriage had been and by textured
I meant bumpy, dropped stitches, amateur darning. I told him

how often you fell in and out of love and how I left and returned
more than once. Perhaps because I didn't care enough, I said.

And perhaps I didn't. There was something he wasn't telling me
but the sun was out and we walked the courtyards and backways

of the neighbourhood, crossed the bridge, watching the sky whiten
and the coloured lamps in the trees come on. We spoke of cities,

their pleasures. The comfort I find in the river. How Brussels' Senne
is covered over, subterranean. Of moving along and clearing out.

Merlin in Mapperley Park

One of the things I was taught about the Metaphysicals
is that they liked to show off to each other, choose
two wildly different things and forge a connection.

I also read that the true measure of useful intelligence,
of creativity, is an ability to see links. And there's been
some talk again about the efficacy of psilocybin

in the treatment of disorders of the brain and surely
that has to be about connections: how these hallucinogens,
so critical to numinous rites (and to my reckless generation),

dissolve boundaries, foster oneness in time, space, fabric,
relevance, an acceptance of one's reassuringly incidental
place in it all. I'm walking down the long hill to the Co-op

for milk and the horrible bread my ancient mother favours
and hold up my phone to identify the twitterings of birds.
Some familiar: blackbird, robin, wren, soothing wood pigeon,

then there's the confusion of greenfinch, goldfinch, dunnock,
great tit, chiff-chaff. Yesterday, thrillingly, in the back garden,
it said great bittern but that must have been the neighbouring boys

drumming. Of course, it raised doubts re the app's accuracy
but I choose to believe and rejoice in the small, plausible birds
in this suburb's trees and hedges. Walking downhill in the mornings

I am likely to cry, which I put down to it being at a time I'd probably
have phoned you to check in while I'm away, when you'd have been
sober, en route to the plot, optimistic for the day's cultivation.

When I whisper to myself that I miss you, it's not entirely true.
It's the potential for things to have been better, the days before
it became so messy. I know so little about birds, the huge song

the flyweight wren produces astonishes me. Proportionately,
I couldn't call so loud. How comforting it is to be irrelevant,
to be as invisible as the landscape, the hawk hanging, the froth

of may or cow parsley, the neat ingenuity of rail-side allotments.
I mean, you see them, but passively. However much I try I can't
make things hang together and yet they do: everything, everything.

Coda: Tips on avoiding the offered consolations of Religion and Therapy

If it's Religion, it'll spot you, even when
you're crouched low behind the credenza.
Better to throw open the door, all breezy,
and announce, 'We're Zoroastrians here.
Welcome to the Fire Temple' and while
Religion fumbles for its specs to Google,
you can shimmy sleekly past, go jog.

Therapy requires acuter acting skills.
Better pretend you're a dog (a Dalmatian,
the least intellectual), then Therapy (all kinds)
will be compelled to fulfil its cracker joke fate
and order you down off the couch, whereupon
you can tail-knock the vase of iris off the table
then lope away, one ear rakishly inside out.

ACKNOWLEDGEMENTS

My thanks go to the editors who first published some of the poems in this pamphlet in *Ink, Sweat and Tears* and *The North*.

'How to be a Widow' won second prize in the Buzzwords Poetry Competition 2024; 'Looking for a cure in parks and gardens' was longlisted in Rialto's Nature and Place Competition 2023; and 'What I do with you now you're dead' was longlisted for the National Poetry Competition 2023.

I am indebted to Mimi Khalvati and Ann and Peter Sansom and to poetry friends who have provided so much kind attention and advice, particularly my glorious Saturday crew, Ramona Herdman, Fokkina McDonnell, Sarah Mnatzaganian, Paul Stephenson and Pam Thompson; and to Jill Abram for her company and encouragement.

And always and in all ways, to our daughters, Ella and Eliza.

ABOUT THE POET

Kathy Pimlott has two pamphlets with The Emma Press: *Goose Fair Night* (2016) and *Elastic Glue* (2019). Her debut full collection, *the small manoeuvres*, was published by Verve Poetry Press (2022). Her work is widely published in magazines and anthologies and she has been longlisted, placed and has won several poetry prizes. She was born and raised in Nottingham but has lived and worked most of her adult life in Covent Garden, specifically Seven Dials, home of the broadsheet and the ballad.

www.kathypimlott.co.uk

ABOUT THE EMMA PRESS

The Emma Press is an independent publishing house based in Birmingham. It was founded in 2012 by Emma Dai'an Wright and has grown to five part-time staff members following support from Arts Council England's Elevate programme in 2020-23.

The Emma Press specialises in poetry, short-form prose and children's books, with translations across all genres. Recent publications have won the Michael Marks Illustration Award (*The Strange Egg*) and been shortlisted for the CLiPPA and the Week Junior Book Awards (*Balam and Lluvia's House*).

In 2024 the Emma Press was a Regional Finalist for Small Press of the Year Award in the British Book Awards, as well as shortlisted for the Independent Publishers Guild's Alison Morrison Diversity, Equity & Inclusion Award.

The Emma Press is passionate about publishing literature which is welcoming and accessible.

Visit our website and find out more
about our books here:
Website: theemmapress.com
Facebook @theemmapress
X @theemmapress
Instagram @theemmapress